THE LITTLE RASCALS STORY BOOK

Adapted by Nancy E. Krulik
from a screenplay written by
Paul Guay & Stephen Mazur &
Penelope Spheeris

UNIVERSAL PICTURES AND KING WORLD PRESENT A PENELOPE SPHEERIS FILM "THE LITTLE RASCALS" ORIGINAL SCORE BY WILLIAM ROSS EDITED BY ROSS ALBERT PRODUCTION DESIGNER LARRY FULTON DIRECTOR OF PHOTOGRAPHY RICHARD BOWEN CO-PRODUCER MARK ALLAN EXECUTIVE PRODUCERS GERALD R. MOLEN DEBORAH JELIN NEWMYER ROGER KING WRITTEN BY PAUL GUAY & STEPHEN MAZUR & PENELOPE SPHEERIS ORIGINAL SOUNDTRACK ON MCA CDs AND CASSETTES PRODUCED BY MICHAEL KING BILL OAKES COMING SOON DIRECTED BY PENELOPE SPHEERIS A UNIVERSAL PICTURE UNIVERSAL AN MCA COMPANY ©1994 UNIVERSAL CITY STUDIOS, INC. & AMBLIN ENTERTAINMENT, INC.

Book designed by Nancy Levin Kipnis

12 11 10 9 8 7 6 5 4   4 5 6 7 8 9/9

Printed in the U.S.A.
First Scholastic printing, September 1994

The members of the He-Man Woman-Haters Club knew something really important was happening. After all, it wasn't every day that Spanky, their leader and president, sent Petey the dog out to track down the members for an emergency meeting.

Once all of the members had given the secret signal and found seats inside the clubhouse, Vice-President Stymie led them in their secret pledge.

The clubhouse was a special place, filled with wagons, dart boards, bicycle wheels, and other special treasures the members had collected from around the neighborhood. Spanky took his place in the front of the room and thanked Petey for his help. Then he prepared to make his big announcement. "Ready to take down the minutes, Uh-Huh?" he asked the boy sitting next to him. "Uh-huh," answered Uh-Huh.

"As you know, I called an emergency meeting today for a very important reason," Spanky said. "This Sunday is the Go-Cart Derby. This Sunday we defend our honor . . . our undefeated streak . . . our trophies!"

The boys looked at *The Blur*, the club's beloved go-cart. *The Blur* was an amazing car — it had never been beaten. Not since the beginning of time — five whole years!

"The reason for the emergency meeting," Spanky continued, "is the choosing of the driver."

"Our driver should be a man who is all he-man," Froggy said, his voice croaking with every word.

Spanky nodded. "Men, our driver is none other than my lifelong chum, my best buddy in the whole wide world — the one, the only . . . Alfalfa!"

Everyone looked around to watch Alfalfa stand and take his bows. But Alfalfa wasn't there!

Alfalfa had missed an emergency meeting of the He-Man Woman-Haters Club. That was bad enough. But even worse, Alfalfa was in the middle of doing the unthinkable — he was singing to a girl . . . in a rowboat!

Alfalfa knew the fellas would be plenty mad at him if they knew he was with a girl. But this wasn't just any girl. This was Alfalfa's darling Darla. Besides, Alfalfa figured, the guys weren't anywhere near the canal.

Alfalfa figured wrong. In fact, all of the He-Man Woman-Haters Club members had left the clubhouse and were now standing on a bridge just above the canal, watching Alfalfa make goo-goo eyes and blow butterfly kisses at Darla!

"This is the most terrible thing that's ever happened in the history of mankind," Buckwheat said.

"But we gotta stick by him," Stymie begged the others. "When a guy's sunk to his rock-bottom lowest, that's when he needs his buddies most." Everyone agreed. They began to plan a way to free Alfalfa from Darla's web of girl magic.

While Spanky and the gang were working out their plan, Butch and Woim, the neighborhood's bullies, were busy building their own go-cart — *The Beast*. "We'll never have to take second to that lunkhead, Spanky, and his friends again," Butch grunted as he put the final wheel on his cart. Clink. Clank. Clunk. As soon as the fourth wheel was on, the other three wheels fell right off. Butch sighed. There was only one way he and Woim were going to beat Spanky's team — they would have to steal *The Blur*.

Alfalfa spent the next morning picking flowers for his ladylove.

"I've come a-courtin'," Alfalfa said, handing her the flowers. "These are for you." Darla beamed at Alfalfa. "They're splendiferous."

Alfalfa puckered up for a big kiss — but, boy, was he in for a surprise. A giant dog leaped out of a limousine and knocked him over. The dog's owner, a rich boy named Waldo, jumped out of the car and smiled at Darla.

"I hope Fifi didn't startle you. She's so playful," Waldo said. Alfalfa looked concerned. He had a feeling Waldo liked his Darla a little too much. Even worse, Darla seemed to like Waldo.

Alfalfa was very relieved when Darla and he were alone once again — and off for a romantic luncheon for two. Even though he had broken one of the Woman-Haters Club rules and brought a girl into the clubhouse, Alfalfa wasn't worried. The guys thought he was at the dentist's with a toothache.

Alfalfa set a beautiful table, complete with candles, on the clubhouse ironing board. "Grape soda?" he offered Darla romantically.

Darla held out her glass. "Fill it to the brim, slim," she said, grinning.

Alfalfa would have been plenty worried if he had realized the other members of the He-Man Woman-Haters Club were spying on him as he dined with Darla. Even Petey and Elmer were in on the action. The guys knew all about Alfalfa's secret date — and they had done a little preparing on their own. They wanted to be certain the date was a disaster!

Darla took a sip of her soda — and spat it out.

"This tastes like it's been strained through an old boot!" she coughed.

Outside, Froggy started to laugh. "Actually, it's a sneaker!" he told Spanky. The guys had replaced all of Alfalfa's carefully prepared food with really disgusting stuff — like sneaker soda and kitty-litter sandwiches. But all the bad food could not keep Alfalfa from his big surprise. Alfalfa had a beautiful ring for Darla.

"I had to eat six boxes of Cracker Jacks to find it," he told her proudly.

Spanky watched in horror as his best pal leaned over and kissed Darla.

"That's it! We've got to put a stop to this right now!" announced the president of the He-Man Woman-Haters Club as he pounded on the club-house door.

Alfalfa jumped up in mid-smooch. The guys were at the clubhouse! He tried to blow out the candles and fold up the ironing board. He hid Darla in the closet and wrapped a napkin over his head — to make it look like he really did have that toothache.

Carefully, Alfalfa opened the clubhouse door. "Hiya, guys! You're back early!" he said with a nervous smile.

"I'd say just in time," Stymie muttered to Spanky. "We're going inside the clubhouse now," he added, trying to push his way past Alfalfa.

Alfalfa started to panic. What if the guys saw Darla? "No, you're not," he said quickly. "I mean, it's such a nice day outside. And heck knows, nothin' goin' on in there."

Spanky sniffed the air. Something smelled like smoke. Alfalfa turned just in time to see smoke coming from inside the clubhouse. Oh no! The clubhouse was on fire! And Darla was stuck in the closet!

But Darla was just fine. But she was so mad at Alfalfa that she drove *The Blur* out of the clubhouse — and right through the back wall!

The Little Rascals got to work putting out the fire. They pelted the clubhouse with water balloons. They poured buckets of water on the flames. Froggy even puffed up his cheeks and tried to *blow* the fire out. In the end, it was President Spanky who grabbed a nearby hose and put out the flames.

The fire was out. But the clubhouse was burned to ashes.

"What horrible force of nature could have caused this disaster?" Spanky cried out. All eyes turned and faced the horrible force — Alfalfa!

"The clubhouse is toast . . . ." Spanky yelled at Alfalfa.

"Now we have no place to go to get away from grown-ups . . . ." Stymie added.

"Our lives are over . . . ." Porky cried.

"And it's all your fault," Spanky finished.

Alfalfa got down on his knees to plead for mercy. "I never knew liking a girl could lead to all of this," he said sadly.

There was only one thing Spanky could do. He sentenced Alfalfa to guard *The Blur* — day and night. And he made Alfalfa vow that he would never speak to Darla again.

The second part would be easy. Alfalfa knew Darla wasn't speaking to him anyway. It was the part about staying out in the open . . . all night . . . all alone . . . that worried Alfalfa.

The gang decided to go easy on him with his guard duty. With Petey as the watchdog, *The Blur* and the boys were safe.

By morning, Alfalfa felt a little better. But no matter how hard he tried, he couldn't forget about Darla. Alfalfa was really sad. Spanky gave him a frog to cheer him up, but even that didn't help. Finally, Spanky decided that it was time for desperate measures. Alfalfa would have to dump that hot tomato in person.

To do that, Spanky and Alfalfa had to visit Darla's dance studio. But on the way they bumped into Butch and Woim who wanted to beat them up — just for fun. In order to slip past the bullies . . . Spanky and Alfalfa went into the studio dressed like ballerinas!

Alfalfa broke into a cold sweat when he saw Darla and her girlfriends.

What if they recognized him while he was dressed in a tutu?

"Hi!" Darla said to the boys. "Who are you?"

Alfalfa was about to say "Alfalfa," but caught himself just in time.

"Al—lice," he said quickly. "Alice Sue Carlotta May Jones. And this is my friend Spankatina."

Whew! That was close!

Luckily, the boys escaped without being discovered.

After that there was no time to think about Darla. Alfalfa and the other Rascals had a clubhouse to rebuild. And to do that, they needed a lot of money. At first, they dressed up like men in long beards and wide-brimmed hats and tried to fool the loan officer at the bank.

When that didn't work, the guys had a new idea. They set up a booth at the county fair. The sign said, "SPANKY'S BELIEVE IT OR ELSE — ONE KWARTER."

Inside the booth, the fellas were all dressed up in funny costumes. They tried to convince their audience that they were silly people, like the Amazing Siamese Twins (born in different parts of the world), the Human Without a Tummy, the Wonder Boy Who Burps the *Battle Hymn of the Republic*, and the Four Foot Man Eating a Chicken.

The audience didn't think the Rascals were very funny. They wanted their money back.

"We have less money than when we came!" Spanky cried out. How would the Rascals ever rebuild the clubhouse?

Then Spanky had a great idea. He convinced Miss Crabtree, a teacher so beautiful even the He-Man Woman-Haters loved her, to put aside all of the money made at the talent-show booth. That money would be the prize money at the go-cart race.

Spanky was sure *The Blur* would win the race. And that the prize money would allow the gang to rebuild the clubhouse.

There was just one problem — while Spanky and the guys were busy at the county fair, Butch and Woim had stolen *The Blur*!

Meanwhile, Darla and Waldo were in the middle of singing a
romantic song when Alfalfa entered the talent-show booth.
Darla wore a red dress and looked into Waldo's eyes as they sang.
It was more than Alfalfa could stand.

Alfalfa knew that Darla could never resist his singing voice.
So there was just one thing for Alfalfa to do. He would have to
sing in the talent show.

Alfalfa went onstage and held up a glass of water. "Let me raise a toast to the girl I love most in the whole world," he said. "Darla." Then he took a sip.

Alfalfa did not know that Waldo had filled the glass with liquid soap. When Alfalfa opened his mouth to sing, all that came out were lots and lots of bubbles!

Late that afternoon, the club members met at the burned-down clubhouse.

"You know, Spanky, I like girls," Alfalfa said. "It might even get worse as I get older."

"I know you like girls, Falf. The problem is, rules is rules." Spanky sighed. "Shoot, without a clubhouse we don't have a club!"

Stymie walked over to Spanky and Alfalfa. He shook his head. "You guys burned down a clubhouse, not a club."

"A club is buddies who stick together no matter what," added Froggy.

"I just wish we could still enter the Go-Cart Derby," Alfalfa said sadly. "But it's impossible."

Spanky grinned. "Who says it's impossible? Every one of us, working together, doing whatever it takes to build the best darn go-cart this town's ever seen — pal, that's all the possible we need!"

And with that, the Rascals went to work building an all-new super-deluxe go-cart, *The Blur 2*! They used things from around the neighborhood — including the washing machine motor from Spanky's house.

By the time Sunday came along, the Rascals were ready. Alfalfa and Spanky looked over the competition. First they saw Butch and Woim's go-cart. It was a vehicle of awe and splendor.

"It looks like *The Blur* with a new paint job," Spanky said. Alfalfa looked at Spanky with surprise. It was *The Blur*!

In the next car over, Alfalfa saw something even worse, that creepy rich kid, Waldo, driving a supersonic sports car. Alfalfa wondered who Waldo's driving partner was.

"Gentlemen, start your engines," the announcer called out.

After a few turns, Waldo had had enough of the
competition. "It's time to lose these losers!" he said.
With the flick of a switch, flames shot out of the back of
his car, and Waldo and his mysterious partner took off at
lightning speed.

Butch and Woim tried to activate the rocket boosters
on their car. But they had put theirs in backwards.
Butch and Woim also took off at lightning speed — but
in reverse!

Waldo was in the lead. But soon Alfalfa and Spanky pulled up
alongside him. Waldo flicked another button. Deadly blades jutted
out from his wheels. Then Waldo drove right toward Alfalfa . . . .

Alfalfa tried to move out of the way. But instead he wound up
heading into oncoming traffic! A truck was heading straight for
them! Immediately Spanky took the wheel and drove directly under
the truck. Luckily the boys ducked — and lived to continue the race.

That was the last straw! Even Waldo's partner couldn't take it anymore, and threw Waldo out of the car . The partner drove off to try to help Alfalfa. It was a good thing, because Butch and Woim were trying one last dirty trick. Butch threw a huge fiery flare onto the Rascals' car!

Spanky and Alfalfa were blinded by smoke from the fire. Waldo's partner drove close to *The Blur 2*, and in a moment of true courage, grabbed the flare and threw it — right onto Butch's lap!

Alfalfa raced to the finish line. The other Rascals were waiting there for him.

"You did it, Alfalfa," Buckwheat cried out. "You won!"

"Now we'll have a clubhouse again!" cheered Porky.

Waldo's partner smiled and took off her helmet. Surprise! It was Darla who had saved the race . . . and the clubhouse!

The Rascals used the prize money to rebuild the clubhouse. Everything went back to being the same as it always was. Except for one little thing. There were new members in the club — Darla and her pal Mary Ann. It looked like the He-Man Woman-Haters Club was going to have to find a new name!